Moose Tooth

written by
Nancy Louise Spinelle
illustrated by
Gloria Gedeon

KAEDEN ❤ BOOKS™

Moose had a loose tooth,
a very loose tooth.

"Boo-hoo!" cried Moose.
"I have a loose tooth."

"Wiggle it out," said a bear.

Moose wiggled and wiggled his tooth, but it wouldn't come out.

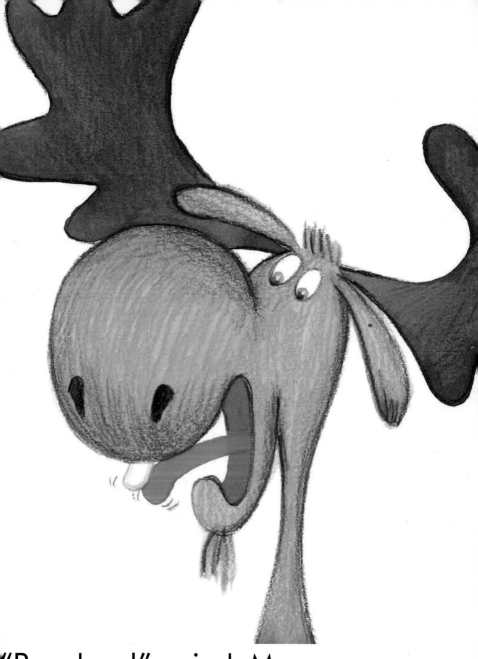

"Boo-hoo!" cried Moose.
"I have a loose tooth."

"Yank it out," said a raccoon.

Moose yanked and yanked his tooth, but it wouldn't come out.

"Boo-hoo!" cried Moose.
"I have a loose tooth."

"Pull it out," said a rabbit.

Moose pulled and pulled his tooth, but it wouldn't come out.

"Boo-hoo!" cried Moose.
"I have a loose tooth."

"Push it out," said a porcupine.

Moose pushed and pushed his tooth. It still wouldn't come out.

12

"Boo-hoo!" cried Moose.
"My tooth is still loose."

"Take a bite of my apple,"
said an owl.

Moose took a bite of the
owl's apple.

14

"Yessss! My tooth came out," shouted Moose.